Things I Like

I Like Basketball

By Meg Gaertner

www.littlebluehousebooks.com

Little Blue House is distributed by North Star Editions:
sales@northstareditions.com | 888-417-0195

Produced for Little Blue House by Red Line Editorial.

Photographs ©: FatCamera/iStockphoto, cover, 8–9, 11; Wavebreakmedia/iStockphoto, 4; monkeybusinessimages/iStockphoto, 7, 16 (bottom right); Aspen Photo/Shutterstock Images, 12–13; Paolo Bona/Shutterstock Images, 15; taka4332/iStockphoto, 16 (top left); Drew Bloksberg/iStockphoto, 16 (top right); fredrocko/iStockphoto, 16 (bottom left)

Library of Congress Control Number: 2019908657

ISBN
978-1-64619-010-2 (hardcover)
978-1-64619-049-2 (paperback)
978-1-64619-088-1 (ebook pdf)
978-1-64619-127-7 (hosted ebook)

Printed in the United States of America
Mankato, MN
012020

About the Author

Meg Gaertner enjoys reading, writing, dancing, and being outside. She lives in Minnesota.

Table of Contents

ball

I Like Basketball

Basketball takes a lot of practice.

We bounce the ball.

My team plays against another team.

35
41
42

We run down the court with the ball.

court

I look at the hoop.

I am going to take a shot.

hoop

I shoot the ball.

I make a basket.

net

My team wins the game.

We like basketball.

BASKET CUP
Pallacanestro - UNDER 11
1^ Classificata
2018/2019

Glossary

ball

hoop

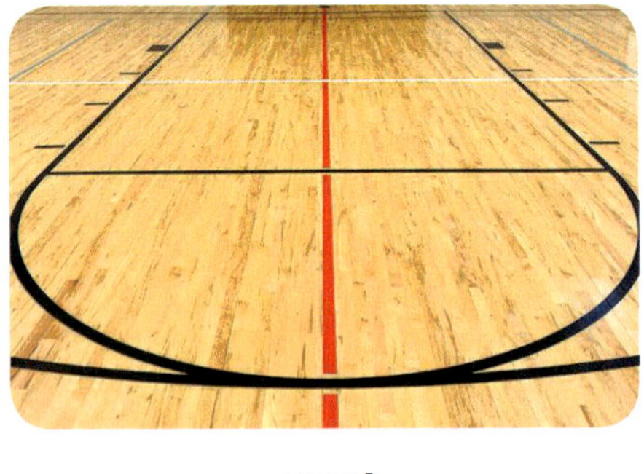

court

team

Index

Things I Like

Some people like dancing or building. Others like cats and dogs. This high-interest series will help young readers explore the things they like.

Books in this series

- I Like Basketball
- I Like Cats
- I Like Dogs
- I Like Horses
- I Like Soccer
- I Like to Build
- I Like to Dance
- I Like to Paint

With simple text, vibrant photos, and high-interest topics, Little Blue Readers are an ideal way for young learners to take their first steps toward literacy.

ISBN: 978-1-64619-049-2

GRL: D

I Got a Pet!

My Pet Hamster

level 2 little blue readers

By Brienna Rossiter